Greenfinger
and Other Mysteries

Stories by
Keith Brumpton, Marjorie Darke
and Jonathan Allen

Illustrated by Keith Brumpton,
Christine Ross and Jonathan Allen

Contents

Greenfinger!

Written and illustrated by
Keith Brumpton

PLANT HEAVEN garden centre
Snakesville, USA.
Tuesday 12 April. 5.05pm.

'Oh, Sheriff,' gasped Mrs Helga Klotz.
'The most dreadful thing has just
happened. I had just popped over to
see my neighbour Mr Hosepipe at his
garden centre when I saw something
out of the corner of my eye. Now my
eyesight ain't too good,' she sobbed,
'but I know what I seen. A runner
bean the size of a bear came from
behind me and grabbed me ... right
here ...'

She pointed to her waist and
sobbed a little more.

'Take your time,' said the Sheriff. 'This is important. You're quite sure this ... giant bean attacked you? Only ... they aren't normally violent.'

'Yes, Sheriff, I'm quite sure. That giant bean is a killer, and it's out there somewhere, waiting to strike again ...'

Spring always came late to the little town of Snakesville. It was near the desert, and the cold night winds kept blowing right over the main street until well into late May.

Holly Wood pulled on an extra sweatshirt, but it didn't stop her shivering. She was peering at the screen of her computer with a troubled look on her face. The screen read:

'GIANT TOMATO TRIED TO SQUASH ME!'

Local doctor, Jim Grubb (47), has described a terrifying ordeal during which he was chased through his home by a giant tomato plant. 'It tried to kill me,' sobbed Dr Grubb, a well-respected member of the town tiddly winks team, and president of the Snakesville Christmas Lights Committee.

Holly paused and looked at the bowl of tomatoes sitting on top of the freezer. It didn't seem possible that a man could be so scared by something so small and round and, er, slow moving.

But then a lot of strange things had been happening in Snakesville just lately. There had been an incident in which two small children claimed to have been followed home by a six-foot cucumber. Another man had been attacked by an over-sized lettuce.

This business with the giant salad sounded pretty fascinating. Holly decided to go and visit her friend Mike. He knew everything there was to know about UFOs and that sort of stuff.

'Come on, Rinty!' shouted Holly, and a scruffy but cheerful looking dog appeared at her side. 'We've got work to do!'

Holly knocked on the door of Mike's trailer. His mum let her in.

'Hi, Holly,' she said. 'Mike's in there watching more Star Trek. It's a wonder that boy hasn't turned into a Vulcan.' Mrs White had a good sense of humour.

Holly knocked on the door to Mike's room. Inside, it looked like aliens had just attacked.

'What's up?' Mike asked, when he saw the serious look on Holly's face. He gave Rinty a scratch behind the ears.

'There's something going on,' began Holly.

'This got anything to do with UFOs?' asked Mike keenly.

'Maybe,' answered Holly, 'but it's mostly to do with vegetables.'

'Vegetables?' Mike's face broke into a smile. 'You're not trying to turn me into a veggie again, are you?'

'No … this is serious … look …'

Six-foot Cucumber Attacks Children

Holly handed Mike a printout from her computer describing all the cases – three in total – of attacks by giant vegetables.

'What d'ya think?' she asked.

Mike gave a low whistle. 'Sounds serious. Guess we should take a look.' Mike looked at the printout again. 'How about we check out the lady who was attacked? Mrs Klotz. I know where she lives. It's next to that garden centre, Plant Heaven.'

```
Police patrol car, Snakesville.
9.30am.
```

Sheriff Eastwood's two-way radio was buzzing with the strangest news.

'Giant beans!' echoed the Sheriff.

'You gotta help us, Sheriff!'

'They're runnin' up and down my garden! Guess they must be runner beans. They look like they mean business!'

But the Sheriff didn't believe all these stories that were coming in. Vegetables didn't attack people, especially not in Snakesville. Snakesville was a quiet little town where nothing much ever happened, or at least that's what they told him when he took the job ...

Sheriff Eastwood decided to head back to his office and go through the paperwork one more time ... maybe he'd missed a clue ... something which would give him some idea of what was going on ...

He passed Darwin's Chemical Factory at the same time as Holly and Mike were roller-blading by in the opposite direction.

Mrs Klotz's home was a pretty pink bungalow with gnomes in the garden.

Mike pressed the bell and waited for Mrs Klotz to appear. It took quite a while because she didn't move too quickly any more, mainly on account of her poor eyesight. Her glasses were as thick as bottle ends.

Rinty wagged his tail and gave Mrs Klotz's hand a lick. Holly and Mike didn't have to ask too many questions before the old lady started spilling out the whole tale.

'It was horrible,' she began. 'I used to watch a lot of horror movies when I was your age, but I never seen anything like that. No siree!'

She continued the story in-between sobs and sips of home-made squash: how the runner bean had slid towards her like some giant snake; how her neighbour, Mr Hosepipe, had bravely run off to call for help; how she'd struggled as the green shoots tightened around her waist, squeezing the very life out of her. Mrs Klotz reached for her smelling salts and seemed too upset to say any more.

'Er, thanks for your help' said Mike abruptly, getting quickly to his feet. 'We'll see ourselves out.'

'Why didn't you listen to the rest of her story?' whispered Holly, as they made their way back down the path.

'Because she's as blind as a bat, and I don't believe a word of it,' answered Mike. 'I mean, did you see those glasses? She wouldn't know a giant bean from a chocolate milkshake!'

Rinty suddenly gave a low growl, which wasn't his style at all.

'Aaaaargh!' A blood-curdling scream echoed from Mrs Klotz's cottage. Holly, Mike and Rinty stopped dead in their tracks.

There was a second, even louder, scream.

'Aaaaaaaaaaaaaaaaaaaaargh!'

Mike raced back to the house. The front door was still open. He reached the dining room just in time to see Mrs Klotz's feet slide out towards the kitchen. They were wrapped in a thick green tendril. As Mike moved to grab her, the plant flicked out another shoot which knocked him to the floor.

'Mike! Mrs Klotz!' cried Holly.

Rinty had begun to howl. By the time Mike had got to his feet again, and Holly had put on Rinty's leash, both the plant and Mrs Klotz had vanished!

A trail of broken shoots and leaves led across the backyard to where Mrs Klotz's glasses lay broken. Mike looked up and down the empty road and scratched his head. 'Killer vegetables! So the old girl was telling the truth after all!'

Holly was as shaken as a cowboy at a rodeo. 'What do we do now?' she stammered.

Mike frowned, looking more serious than she'd ever seen him. 'We go and see the Sheriff. This is out of our league, kid.'

Police HQ, Snakesville. 12.10pm.

Sheriff Eastwood was not a big man, but he had a big moustache. And right now he felt like hiding behind it. The phone hadn't stopped ringing all morning and he had enough paperwork to wallpaper his house with. And now these two crazy kids were wasting his time with another story about giant vegetables invading the town.

'You kids watch too much TV!'

'But, Sheriff, we were there when it happened!'

Just then Sheriff Eastwood's radio crackled into life.

'Eastwood here. What's new?'

'Got another Killer Veggie for you,' came the voice of Deputy Dimkin. 'We got a call from Darwin's Chemical Factory. Can you take a look?'

'What is it this time ...' growled the Sheriff, rolling his eyes, 'a couple of psycho carrots on the loose?'

He turned to Holly and Mike. 'Don't waste my time any more ... you hear me?'

'Where are we going?' asked Holly, as they roller-bladed down the High Street.

'The chemical factory,' answered Mike. 'You heard the Sheriff's radio. Sounds like there's been another sighting there.'

Holly had always hated the chemical factory. It pumped out big clouds of green gases day and night, and when the wind was in the wrong direction, it made the town smell worse than a roomful of skunks. She wondered if there might be some connection between the chemical plant and all these giant vegetables.

Mike and Holly arrived at the factory and headed straight for the main office. On their way in they passed old Mr Hosepipe from the garden centre, whose granddaughter worked at the factory.

'Hi, Mr Hosepipe,' smiled Holly,

but he walked straight past her without stopping.

Mike pointed to a sign marked 'Reception', and it wasn't long before they were standing before Darius Darwin, general manager of the factory.

'Sorry, kids, but I'm very busy. Can you make this quick?'

Holly couldn't think of a good reason for being in the factory, but Mike started telling some tale about doing a school project on the effect of chemicals upon local plants. It was a good story, but Mr Darwin didn't seem too keen to start a discussion.

'Let me have it in writing,' he snapped. 'I'll see what I can do. The chemicals we use are good for the environment. We pride ourselves on being green.'

'Green! The only green thing in this factory is the smog it pumps out,' thought Holly, angrily.

They had said goodbye to Mr

Darwin and were on their way out when Mike happened to look back at Mr Darwin's office. To his amazement, a huge object had suddenly appeared behind Mr Darwin. It looked like a giant radish. Rinty began growling again.

Even though they raced back to the office, leaping the stairs two at a time, they were still too late to save Mr Darwin. The giant radish swallowed him whole then raced off into the distance faster than you'd imagine a root vegetable could ever travel …

22 Clinton Street, Snakesville. 4.15pm.
Holly stared at her computer and did another word search. She typed in 'giant vegetables' and then watched as the results came up on the screen. Something near the bottom of the page caught her eye.

The Snakesville Express 21 September

LOCAL MAN COMPLAINS AFTER BEST VEGETABLE CONTEST

Angry gardener, Mr Larry Hosepipe, has lashed out at the judges who awarded him second prize in the September Snakesville Prize Vegetable Show. 'Size ain't everything,' snapped Hosepipe (68). 'Quality counts too.' He said he would be taking the matter further. Judge Darius Darwin said the whole incident was sour grapes, or should I say, 'sour vegetables'.

A hunch began to form in Holly's mind. She called Mike, and within minutes he had arrived at her house.

PLANT HEAVEN garden centre, Snakesville. 5.00pm.

The locals called Larry Hosepipe 'Greenfinger', and the old man certainly had a way with plants. His nursery was a gardener's dream. It had everything from roses to runner beans. You name it and 'Plant Heaven' would have it.

But was it just Holly's imagination or did all the plants in 'Plant Heaven' seem quite a bit bigger than normal?

'It's just your imagination,' answered Mike, but before he could say anything else, Rinty's barking alerted them to an old man dressed in dungarees and carrying a pair of shears. On either side of him were two of the biggest courgettes Holly had ever seen.

'Can I help ya?' snorted the man.

It was Greenfinger himself.

'Let's not beat about the bush,' began Mike. 'We think you might know something about the giant vegetables that have been attacking our town.'

Greenfinger's eyes grew wide as flying saucers and his lips curled into an ugly sneer.

'Oh, I know about it all right. They're my vegetables you see.'

'They obey my commands and my commands alone!'

'He's nuts!' thought Holly, preparing to run for it. But before either of them could move, Greenfinger turned to his courgettes and yelled, 'Seize them!'

The courgettes moved forwards. Things were looking bad until Rinty suddenly leapt in front of Holly and grabbed Greenfinger by the seat of his dungarees. This seemed to confuse the courgettes and they backed off into the distance.

Greenfinger managed to shake
Rinty off and then retreated toward
his row of greenhouses. 'See how you
fare against my Killer Tomatoes!' he
laughed, like some madman from a
James Bond film.

While Holly called for the Sheriff, Mike and Rinty raced after Greenfinger. A three-metre tall sprout rolled past them and they had to dive for cover. Holly, meanwhile, was trying to dodge an angry sweetcorn with slithering husks.

'Sheriff Eastwood! This is an emergency! No fooling!'

Greenfinger was cornered in the last greenhouse but he didn't seem worried. 'I'm sure you've eaten lots of tomatoes, but never imagined that one day a tomato would eat you!' he laughed madly.

Taking its cue, the tomato lurched forward, ready to attack Mike. Mike sprang to one side and grabbed hold of a nearby garden hose lying coiled on the ground.

Mike fired a jet of water straight at the tomato. The force of the spray dislodged a giant slug curled on top of the tomato. It fell with a loud 'SPLAT!' right on to Greenfinger.

'Aaaargh!' the old man screamed, as the hungry slug set to work.

Mike tried to tackle the slug but there wasn't anything he could do. By the time Sheriff Eastwood arrived it was too late for Greenfinger.

Searching through Mr Hosepipe's office, the Sheriff later told them how he'd uncovered the rest of the old man's crazy plan: he had fed his plants with chemicals from Darwin's

Chemical Factory, stolen by his granddaughter. He then genetically engineered them, developing a whole race of giant vegetables ready to obey his every command.

'Revenge is a dirty word,' the Sheriff told Holly and Mike. 'Remember the Prize Vegetable Show? Well, Greenfinger wanted revenge on those judges who'd awarded him second prize in the show. Only trouble was he lost control of his vegetables and they began to develop minds of their own.'

'So you don't reckon he planned on killing Mrs Klotz?' asked Holly.

'No. In the end, Mr Darwin was the only judge the plants managed to kill. And then they turned on old Greenfinger himself ...'

'That's what happens when you mess with nature!' added Mike, with a shake of the head.

The biggest plants were rounded up and placed in a secure home.

Within a few weeks of being looked after with tender love and care, they returned to their usual size and were allowed back into the community.

'Still gonna be a vegetarian?' Mike asked Holly, as they rode home in the Sheriff's car.

'That's a tough one,' she laughed. 'Though the tomato is a fruit and not a vegetable you know …'

Just then Sheriff Eastwood's radio burst into life.

'Sheriff?' called Deputy Dimkin. 'We got a report of an old lady says her pet rabbit got abducted by aliens.'

The Sheriff shook his head angrily. 'They told me this was a QUIET town!'

Holly threw Mike a quick smile. The Sheriff had a lot to learn …

In the Middle of the Night

Written by Marjorie Darke
Illustrated by Christine Ross

'Ghosts come back to haunt farmyards where they lived,' Tom told Kate as they ate their supper. 'I mean cow-ghosts and sheep-ghosts. Ours do. And I've seen a shepherd with no head. So don't look out of your window tonight.'

Kate stared at her brother. What was he on about? He'd always said ghosts were just stories.

'Why not?' She wasn't going to let on she felt scared.

He flapped his arms, pushing his face into hers. 'They'd see you and fly up – whoosh ... straight through you!'

'That's not funny, Tom,' Mum snapped. 'You'll give her nightmares.'

Nightmares came anyway without Tom's ghosts.

In bed, Kate buried her head under the duvet. It was the awful silence that made bad dreams. Their farm had always been full of noises – moos and baaing, old Bess barking. Then the horrible foot-and-mouth disease came. Many of their cows and sheep and those on farms around became ill, and men with guns arrived to stop it spreading. They destroyed

every animal – sick, healthy – they all
had to be shot. Now Bess was dead as
well … not from foot-and-mouth but
old age. Even Tilly, the cat, had
disappeared.

'She'll come back,' Mum said.

Kate didn't believe her. Missing the
animals was like having toothache.

The night wasn't cold but she
shivered. If she kept her eyes open,
she might stay awake and not dream?
It must be morning soon …

Sounds of breakfast dishes clattering on the kitchen table came up the stairs. Tom's feet went rushing down. Mum shouted, 'Get a move on, Kate! You won't have time for breakfast!'

Kate's eyes felt sticky with sleep. She didn't want to go to school. She didn't want to stay at home.

'KATE!' Mum shouted.

'I heard,' Kate yelled, getting up. In a funny way the shouts were better than too much quiet.

She hunted for her favourite old green jersey. Not in any drawer. Not in her cupboard. Other clothes tumbled out.

'KATE! YOU'LL MISS THAT BUS!'

Scrambling into school clothes, Kate slid down the banisters. Her baby brother (Timothy Ivor Grant, Tig for short) was banging his spoon as she went into the kitchen.

'Great noise!' she said, helping herself to cornflakes.

Dad was stacking the dishwasher.
She still wasn't used to seeing him do
this. He always used to be first up and
out milking.

Tig was quiet now, wiping bread
and sticky jam round his tray and
mouth. Kate stuffed in the last
cornflake.

'Mum, where's my bus pass?'

'On the dresser,' Mum said.

Kate looked. 'Not there.'

'Of course it is!'

' 'Tisn't!'

'Use your eyes! I put it there. Don't get in a temper.' Mum was in a bit of a temper herself. 'Hurry up. Tom has gone.'

Dad closed the dishwasher. 'Mustn't miss the bus, chick. It won't hang about today. Not after yesterday.'

He meant the accident outside their farm. A lorry had run into a deer.

He took money from his pocket. 'Get a ticket … any left over, buy some crisps!'

'Thanks, Dad!'

'You spoil that child, Dan,' Mum grumbled. 'She's always losing things.'

Not fair, Kate thought – things hid themselves. Like Tig's baby bottle with the blue top. And Dad's big torch that had disappeared. Stuffing feet into wellingtons, grabbing shoes and schoolbag, she ran across the silent empty farmyard. Tom had already tramped over the disinfectant straw mat which was supposed to stop the disease spreading. He had gone through the gate and was climbing on to the bus.

'Wait for me!' Stamping over the mat, she hopped about kicking off her boots.

The bus driver revved his engine. 'Hurry up! I haven't got all day.'

Kate didn't bother with shoelaces.

'Mind out,' he said, as she tripped on the steps. She paid for her ticket and, as the bus lurched away, fell into the only empty seat – next to Tom, which was a pain. She wanted to sit by her friend Lisa and join in the chat and giggling.

Tom was frowning back at the farm.

'What you staring at?' Kate asked.

No answer.

'Bet you've forgotten something!'

'It's not me that has a hole for a brain,' he snapped.

Kate squeezed up her eyes. Staring through the window she tried to fill the empty fields with cows and sheep. But Tom's shoulders got in the way. Nothing was right since the animals were shot. To cheer herself up she counted the leftover money in her hand. There wasn't enough for crisps.

The day didn't get any better at school. And it's Friday, she thought gloomily on the way home. A whole weekend stuck on the farm. No meeting friends. No sleepover with Lisa. The wood was out of bounds. Fields and footpaths were closed.

Tom was no use. After tea she asked if they could play his Tomb-Raider game.

'Can't,' he said. 'Got loads of homework,' and took himself off.

Mum came in, Tig crawling after her. 'Have you seen the milk powder? I want to make up Tig's bottle.'

Kate shook her head.

'Don't say *that* has gone missing as well!' She picked up Tig who had begun to grizzle.

Rain pattered on the window. Even the weather was down in the dumps!

That night Kate woke with a start. A thin line of light showed between the curtains. It shivered on the floor, then went out, as if someone had switched off the moon. She knew it was only a cloud, but pulled the duvet up to her chin, listening. No wind rustling the trees. Even the rain had stopped. What had disturbed her? Tom's ghosts? Suppose the shepherd with no head was out there now, rounding up the ghost-sheep? Kate's heart bumped against her ribs. But how could he see with no eyes?

Getting out of bed she went to the window.

Her bedroom was above the farmyard. There were barns on two sides. A stable. A hedge. A fence with a gate. The gate led into a field next to a little river. On the other side were more fields. A small wood climbed a hill not far from the road.

But that was in daylight. This was night-time. Her legs wanted to run back to bed.

'Look NOW!' she said fiercely, opening her eyes wide.

Not a ghost-sheep or ghost-cow in sight! Thin mist curled round shadows that seemed to wave at her. At the same moment a stair tread squeaked like an explosion.

Kate froze. Ghosts glided, didn't they? Ghosts didn't make stairs squeak. Faint shuffling sounded from the kitchen. Then the moon came from behind a cloud. Down in the farmyard a thicker shadow moved. A coat-shaped shadow ... with *no head*!

Bolting across the landing into Tom's bedroom, she hissed, 'Tom, wake up. We've got ghosts ... and burglars!'

She tried to shake him but there was nothing under the duvet. About to run to Mum and Dad, she saw the coat-shape again, in her head. She knew that shape – Tom's dressing gown with its hood up! Tom had to be underneath.

Back in her bedroom she pulled on jeans and jersey. Going downstairs, the same tread squeaked. She held her breath. Gentle snoring came from Mum and Dad's room – nothing else. In the kitchen the back door was not locked. Dad's torch was still missing. To switch on the light was too much of a risk. She felt for her boots … found them … and opened the door.

Outside, her friendly farmyard had disappeared. No moon. No stars. No anything. She thought of her warm bed then stepped into the black wall.

Slowly crossing the farmyard, her eyes got used to the dark. Creepy shadows played games. Long fingers beckoned. Faces grinned. But there were no ghost-animals – not even a tiny ghost-lamb. Kate felt a bit disappointed. Then a twig of hedge scratched her cheek.

She squeaked. Jumped. Kicked something hard. Tried not to fall over. Crashed against the stable door, and fell in. The din was awful!

As she hit the floor, two glowing eyes stared into hers. 'You great nit!' Tom's voice hissed.

Light beamed at her.

Kate squeezed up her eyes. She saw Dad's torch in his hand.

Tom waved it at her. 'Why are you here? It's the middle of the night!'

She got to her knees. 'Can't see!'

Pointing the torch at the ground, he shut the door with his foot. In his other hand was Tig's missing bottle.

There was a scrabbling sound.

'What's that?' she gasped.

'What d'you think!' Still mad at her, he knelt and put the torch on the ground. In the ray of light, Kate saw a tiny animal wobbling on long thin legs. It had white spots on its back and a dark stripe running into its little tail.

Not a ghost-lamb. A real live fawn! Very gently she stroked it. The

fawn trembled. 'Where did you find it?'

'In our field near the road,' Tom
said. 'Its mum was that dead deer.'

'We aren't supposed to go into the
field.'

'So what! I looked through my
binoculars and there it was, lying in
the grass waiting. Couldn't let it die of
hunger, could I?'

Kate stroked the fawn again,
remembering the men with guns.
'D'you think they'll let us keep it?'

Before Tom had time to answer, footsteps sounded outside. The stable door opened. Dad stood there, holding up the old storm lamp.

Nobody spoke.

At last Dad said, 'Indoors – all of you!'

Tom put down the bottle and picked up the fawn. Kate picked up the bottle and what seemed to be a little blanket Tom had used to make a bed for the fawn.

Mum was in the kitchen wearing her dressing gown and a frown.

Before she could speak, Kate burst out, 'Itsmumisdeadcanwekeepit?'

Mum and Dad looked at each other. Then they both looked at Fawn.

'*Please*!' Kate begged.

'You know what happened to our cows and sheep,' Dad reminded her. 'We have to go by the foot-and-mouth rules.'

'But not tonight, Dan,' Mum said quickly. 'We'll make up a bed in the kitchen for the poor little thing. Give us that blanket, Kate.'

The blanket turned out to be her old green jersey. Kate didn't mind. She gave Mum Tig's bottle.

'So that's where it went!'

'And the baby milk,' Tom said. 'Fawn guzzled the lot.'

They put the jersey in a cardboard box with a hot water bottle tucked underneath. Then they went to bed.

Next morning Kate heard the postman's van drive away. In the old days Bess barked when he came. No Bess now. No Tilly either. She pulled the duvet over her head … remembered Fawn, and scrambled out.

Down in the kitchen Dad was opening letters. Tig was in his high chair, guzzling milk. But Kate saw she was too late to feed Fawn. Tom was holding the blue-topped bottle.

Mum noticed Kate was cross. 'Cheer up! Take a look in that box by the fire.'

Not wanting to, Kate did. There,

lying on top of some old newspapers, was a heap of fur.

'Tilly!' Kneeling down she saw it wasn't just Tilly. Five tiny kittens nuzzled into their mum's fur.

'She must have come through the cat flap last night and found the box by the fire,' Mum said. 'Feed her, Kate. She must be hungry. And give her a saucer of milk as a treat.'

As Kate put two saucers on the floor, Tilly stretched, purring, and began to lap. The kittens fell in a

squeaking heap.

Kate smiled. Animal noises – like old times!

Dad had opened another letter. 'Hey, what about this!' He waved it like a flag. 'Says here that tomorrow all footpaths are to open again!'

'Does that mean we can have cows and sheep?' Tom asked eagerly.

'Not yet, but it won't be long.'

Lifting the teapot, Mum smiled.

Kate waited.

'Best news for months!' Dad sat down at the table.

Kate tried to catch Tom's eye.

Mum poured tea. Dad stirred in sugar. Tom helped himself to cornflakes.

Kate couldn't wait any longer. 'What about Fawn? Can we keep her?' She held her breath.

Dad put down his cup. 'I don't see why we shouldn't. Not forever mind, but until she can take care of herself … if you two promise to look after her.'

Tom and Kate grinned at each other.

'Course we will,' Tom promised.

'Then we can take her to the wildlife park down the road. She'll be safe there.' Dad sat back in his chair. 'And Kate ... no more losing things. Have you found that bus pass yet?'

'Ah!' said Mum, her face rather pink. 'In the dresser drawer, where I'd popped it for safe keeping!'

The Case of the One-Legged Kangaroo

Written and illustrated by
Jonathan Allen

'Help!' screamed Mrs Goose. 'Thieves! Robbers! Burglars! I've been robbed! He-e-e-lp!'

Amateur investigator Damien Duck pricked up his ears. Well, he would have done if ducks had those kind of ears … He turned his head sharply toward the noise.

'Burglars!' he exclaimed. 'This sounds like a job for Damien Duck, Amateur Investigator! Come on Borage, get your skates on! Our burglar-detecting skills are urgently needed!' Borage was Damien Duck's assistant, a small, anxious-looking anteater with a large hat.

'Right behind you, Boss,' cried Borage, 'just give me a minute to go and get me skates ...'

'Borage,' sighed Damien Duck, 'I wasn't talking about real skates.'

'But real skates are the only kind of skates I've got ...' muttered Borage.

'Burglars! Thieves! Video stealers!' Mrs Goose was still screaming, fit to bust. Damien Duck and Borage cut short their discussion of skates, real or otherwise, and rushed round the corner to where Mrs Goose was having hysterics on the pavement.

'My video recorder has been stolen!' she wailed. 'My lovely new video recorder! My beautiful, shiny, brand spanking new video recorder, gone! My wonderful, gleaming …'

'Mrs Goose! Pull yourself together!' Damien Duck interrupted her. 'We're here to help you get it back! Now, first of all, what does it look like?'

'Get it back?' quavered Mrs Goose. 'Get it back? Get back my lovely, marvellous, fabulous …'

'Yes, Mrs Goose!' replied Damien Duck. 'But to help us get it back, you will need to answer some questions. Please try to concentrate. What does the stolen video recorder look like?'

'Is it one of those new silver ones with NICAM stereo and video plus?' asked Borage enthusiastically. 'The one that links up to a computer and lets you set the timer eight years in advance and has one of those surround sound thingies and …?'

'Borage!' warned Damien Duck, 'I ask the questions if you don't mind.' He turned to Mrs Goose. 'Now, Mrs Goose, think carefully, is it one of those silver ones with NICAM stereo and video plus? One that links up to a computer and lets you set the timer eight years in advance and has one of those surround sound thingies …?'

'Yes,' sobbed Mrs Goose, 'but you forgot to mention the Teletext with optional Chinese subtitling, and how you can link it up to no less than fourteen widescreen digital TVs anywhere between four and ...'

'OK, OK!' said Damien Duck, stopping her in mid flow. 'We get the idea. Now that we know what kind of video recorder it is, we know what to look out for. Next, we need to find out how the burglar got in.'

'Through the front room window,' said Mrs Goose. 'I left it open. I mean, it's such a hot day and my house gets so stuffy unless I open the window in the front room. It's not so bad in the kitchen since I got one of those fan things that sucks the bad air out but ...'

'Can you show us the window, please?' Damien Duck cut in. Mrs Goose pointed to a nearby open ground floor window.

'That one. The one with the bent catch. I've told my Ronald a thousand times about that, but he just says …'

Damien Duck strode purposefully over to the window and examined it. Then he bent down and examined the flowerbed in front of the window.

'Aha!' he exclaimed. 'Borage, come and look at this. Look at the flowerbed and tell me what you see.'

Borage peered at it. 'Three dandelions, four sunshine daisies, some stones, lots of earth, obviously, and something that might be a crocus but it's hard to tell with that footprint being there. The poor thing's been squashed flat ...'

Damien Duck sighed again.

'Not the flowers, you fool. The footprint! Now, who do you suppose the footprint belongs to?'

Borage pondered.

'Probably Mrs Goose,' he replied. 'Seeing as it's in her front garden, but if you want it, just ask her nicely, I'm sure she'll let you have it.'

'I meant who made it?' said Damien Duck, through his clenched beak.

'Why, do you want them to make you one?' Borage sounded confused.

'No I don't!' shouted Damien Duck. 'It was made by the burglar as he climbed down from the window sill. It's a clue!'

'Ah,' said Borage.

Damien Duck shook his head. As a detective's assistant, there were times when Borage was about as much use as a teapot to a goldfish.

A short distance away from the flowerbed was a small pile of rubbish. Damien Duck examined it excitedly.

'Look, Borage, more clues.' He took out his notebook. 'Four empty soft drink cans, twelve crisp packets and an old sock with a large hole in the toe, grey,' he muttered, noting it all down.

'And just look at this!' said Damien Duck, pointing excitedly at a second flowerbed. 'Another footprint! And it's exactly ...' He paced out the distance between the two footprints ... 'exactly four metres away from the first one.'

He called Mrs Goose over to look. She had recovered somewhat from her hysterics. Damien Duck pointed out the footprints.

'You know what this means, Mrs Goose?' She shook her head and opened her mouth to speak.

'It means', explained Damien Duck quickly, 'that the burglar must have very, very long legs if one foot landed here, and another foot landed four metres away here. You don't have any burglar giraffes around here, do you?'

Mrs Goose looked from one footprint to the other and shook her head once more.

'Not that I've seen,' she said. 'But there's this dreadful stoat family at number fourteen, they ...'

'Pity,' said Damien Duck, 'because if you had, and if he was found to be covered in bits of crisp, from having eaten twelve packets of crisps, he would almost certainly be your burglar.'

'Boss,' said Borage, thoughtfully. 'You know, I don't reckon it could have been a giraffe, I mean, how's a giraffe going to open a packet of crisps? What with him having hooves and not fingers.'

Damien Duck considered. 'Hmm, good point, Borage,' he admitted, 'unless the giraffe has an assistant, another animal who goes wherever he goes and whom he uses to open his crisps for him, but I don't think that's very likely. Well … it just goes to show that even great minds like mine can jump to the wrong conclusion once in a very long while. So what's your theory?'

'Well …' said Borage, 'I was wondering about a kangaroo perhaps being your burglar. He made the footprints hopping away with the video. Trouble is, he'd have to be a one-legged kangaroo, as there's only one print for each hop.'

'Unless …' put in Damien Duck, 'unless he had both feet in one boot to put us off the scent. Cunning creatures kangaroos! He steals the video, stuffs it into his pouch, all the while munching bag after bag of crisps, and hops away.'

'Don't forget the fizzy drink, Boss,' Borage reminded him.

'Ah, yes, the fizzy drink.' Damien Duck narrowed his eyes. 'The crisps were to keep his energy up for the long getaway hops he had to do and the drink was to wash down the crisps.'

'And the single sock was left behind because he only needed one sock for both feet in the one boot. Two socks made too much of a tight fit,' added Borage.

'Tremendous!' declared Damien Duck. 'All the police have to do is find a crisp-covered kangaroo, smelling of cheese and onion, hopping at high speed with both legs in one boot, with a video recorder stuffed down his pouch.'

'And he'd be burping a lot,' put in Borage, 'with all that fizzy drink inside him and all that hopping about. But there's one thing bothering me.'

'What would that be?'

'Where's the other boot? Did he hop all the way here in one boot, or did he discard the other one after stealing the video recorder? And if so, where is it?'

Damien Duck considered. 'This kangaroo is obviously a desperate character ...' he declared, 'one who would stop at nothing in the pursuit of his life of crime. One who would think it no disgrace to steal a single boot from outside a shoe shop, where, as you know, only single boots are displayed to discourage criminals, who in the normal course of events would require no less than two boots, a left and a right!' Borage gasped.

'Yes, Borage!' continued Damien Duck. 'A desperate criminal indeed! One the police should take all possible measures to apprehend!'

'Talking of which ...' murmured Borage, stepping hurriedly back as a large policeman came dashing towards them along the pavement.

'Gangway, ladies and gents!' he was shouting, 'I am in hot pursuit of a thief!'

'Aha! Here are the police now,' said Damien Duck, stepping forward. 'Good to see you, Officer … Urk!'

Borage pulled him back just in time to prevent him being flattened by the oncoming officer of the law.

The policeman flashed past them, skidded to a halt, then suddenly launched himself into the bushes beside Mrs Goose's house. There was the sound of a scuffle, a cry of, 'You're nicked!' Then he emerged, slightly dishevelled and breathing heavily, clutching a new-looking silver video recorder. The kind that has video plus, NICAM stereo and optional Chinese subtitling, etc, etc.

Behind him, handcuffed to his other wrist, trailed a sullen-looking cat. 'I've got your video recorder and I've got your burglar, Mrs Goose!' panted the policeman. 'A cat burglar no less. This cat was seen sneaking through your garden carrying your video recorder. I knew he wouldn't get far carrying a silver video recorder. The kind that has video plus, NICAM stereo and ...'

'That's fantastic!' cried Mrs Goose. 'Well, who would have believed it? Thank you so much, Officer. My lovely video recorder! Safe! Isn't that wonderful, Mr Duck? ... Mr Duck?'

But Damien Duck was already out of sight round the street corner, heading homeward with Borage hurrying after him.

'I've just thought of something, Boss,' Borage was saying. 'For a minute, I thought they'd got the wrong animal, but what about this for a theory? The reason the footprints were so far apart was because of all that pavement. The burglar probably took loads of steps between them but we could only see his footprints where the ground was soft. And maybe the dustmen dropped that rubbish. Perhaps a bag split or something. What do you think, Boss? Boss?'

For once Damien Duck, Amateur Investigator, kept his mouth shut.